# TRAITOROUS TRADERS

Charles Rhodes Jamison

Generations ago arose the oceans dawning a new world. Those with knowledge of the sea controlling a vessel rode out a 21st century deluge. The highest peaks of land has given some sort of refuge to people struggling for survival. A population grows more desperate as resources dwindle and legend tells a natural nirvana exists on the outskirts. Only Shelly Jibson and her motley crew of three have the means to travel far and wide; causing friction among others who all want a piece of the pie.

*Dedicated to you the reader.*

On an always sunny day, as usual the morning tide washes ashore a starfish. White sand, turquoise water brings about easy stillness here on this remote island. Until the bow of a wooden ship demolishes a crustacean. Big brown boots alight crushing what's left of the starfish. Thick mucus hits the pristine beach. The first man to exit the boat wears a long jacket. He spits again. The other two have tattered clothes, both weathered and tired.

All three pause on shore assessing surrounding. Big brown boots man goes ahead. One shouts to leader, "Ah hoy, what now?" Without turning back, tilting his head upward and to the right, in a loud response moving quickly forward; the spitter sputters, "Wait for Luna to show her face!"

The two staying behind (Tim and Jim) begin securing the boat while displaying their bond. Tim throws rope. Jim catches thrown rope. Jim jams stake into ground. Tim drives it deeper with hammer pound. Boat ship shape, safe on shore. Tim tosses Jim a pebble. Jim launches that back in water. The two laugh and idly catch up following the leader by precedent and sputum.

Stomping onwards the boss slashes foliage aggressively till children hastily encounter. The terrain opens up as the big brown boots man debushes. He pushes playful children aside to make his way. A child buttonholes his long jacket. He insensitively smacks the little hand even shoving adjoining shoulder. The poor kid falls to the ground but the boy smiles, picks himself up, dusts himself off then admires the button he just copped.

The youthful crowd circles around. The boy holds the brown button up high for the sun to see, at that moment all children exclaim and stretch the "o" in "wow." The man's sudden presence freezes a village of roughly fifty.

A swarthy young girl darts from the crowd and blazes through a trail of shrubs. She knows these woods, every rock and each tree. Her quickness, agility astounds any viewer. Before arriving on the other side of the small island, she scoops up an acorn with her foot, kicking it upwards to catch with her hand - then bashing it against the last rock of the inner terrain. She shoves the nut in her mouth while approaching a woman on shore. Slowing down now she swallows the final bit, takes a breath and a look around.

The female lying half in the sand, other half in the calm water speaks first,

"Hey Mina."

Mina has mocha matted hair joined with the most precious face. She kicks the sand prior to uttering, "That Dick is here." The sorrel haired lady laughs correcting Mina, "Richard, only I call him Dick."

"Okay, fine... Richard is here."

The woman stands up next to a canoe. She states aloud,

"His name could also be Trouble."

Talking sweetly now, Mina gazes up putting her hand on the grown up's leg asking, "How are you today Shelly?"

"Oh fine, let's see what the trouble is."

The two trot along the shore line side by side making their way back. Similar to a mean bear, big brown boots man fires out of the shrubs and onto the sand. He points directly at Shelly, communicating maliciously,

"Shelly Jibson, How do you do doll?"

"Okay for now. What brings you here today, Richard?"

Mina disappears into the woods. Richard expectorates on the sandy beach. Gross for Shelly to view, worse for the crab below,

"The goods, always for your goods. You should be familiar with this dance. You and Preston have what the village needs. I require all I desire, so as usual I inquire, when are you and Preston going to show me The Island of The Beast? Then we can truly dance."

He continues...   "Who will be disquieting Preston, me or you?"

Mina comes back briskly accompanying several children. The young crowd stays back but Mina runs past Richard to sit in eager anticipation by the canoe. Mina grabs hold of a rope attached to the sea vessel. She waits, stares at Shelly for approval. Shelly rubs her forehead using her wrist and backside of hand. She throws Mina a regretful point. Mina pulls the rope. The line jumps as opposite end goes in oceanic water. Mina rings Preston's submerged bell. Her eyes wide open, Mina stares at the water. About five seconds go by then the water swirls from whom the bell tolls. The swirl becomes a vortex advancing to shore. A wet grown man surfaces, shaking off like a dog. This male moves slowly and pauses once out of water. He waves to Mina with both hands. He does that welcoming gesture until he meets Mina and grabs both of her hands gently. He talks softly, "Wolf?" The pair walks toward Shelly and Richard. As they stroll Preston grooms Mina's head. The usual picking, flicking and pulling, Mina even once smacks Preston's hand but he always continues no matter sundry swats. This semi-aquanaut wears animal skin, hung out to dry on the canoe. Shelly meets the two halfway. Preston gives Shelly an oyster. Richard shouts twenty yards away, "What's that?" Shelly makes a raspberry at such a comment. Meaning with help from her mouth, an exhalation of disdainful air propels a sound of contempt. She murmurs to herself, "Son of a prick." She tucks the oyster within her waistband.

Shelly dresses the same as Preston. They drape animal skin on themselves and secure with rope....they make it work. The three stand side by side (Mina in the middle). They make the same gesture at Richard. Their palms up, shoulders shrugged and brows perked gesticulating, "What, you annoying nat?" Preston breaks the ice, "How are you feeling today, Richard? Nice weather huh?"

The children are lurking on the outskirts of this meeting. They wave over to other curious villagers. Richard flings his leather coat backwards below his belt. He places both hands at his sides and shows an angry glare at Preston. Richard verbalizes,

"Yeah, yeah, yeah. Your politeness is always a delay. Preston, I am thirsty and hungry. I am tired of this discourteous discourse we have. Your suavity is of no courtesy to me, my men nor your village." Preston takes one step toward Richard,

"My village. Well I'll be. Shelly, Mina did you hear? Well hot dog… sounds like we have been given a village. Dick, I knew it was good to see you today. This is great news."

The Villagers laugh amongst themselves. Richard raises his voice,

"All of you laugh now. Soon your throats will dry, your stomachs will wither because your stand-up comedian here is a selfish tyrant." Preston sighs,

"Richard, we have been over this. We can not deplete the island of all resources by bringing the entire crop." Richard slowly stomps at Preston and gets in his face,

"This is why we should take it. Take it for yourself and take it for us. Your father would have. Your father almost did."

Preston places two fingers on Richard's chest,

"That's enough. Stop right there. Tomorrow I go. I stock up and this is how long it will continue for as long as we know each other. My loyal peer, Shelly, will take only what is needed and nothing more. Appears to me, Dick, you have a problem and I am not your solution."

Mina brings two wooden shot glasses of water handing those to Preston. Preston accepts from Mina, Preston continues, "Please quench your thirst now. Tomorrow we shall have more, Cheers." Richard slaps Preston's hand and tosses his shot of water in Mina's direction. Preston lowers his head and turns his back on Richard and begins strutting away, "Goodbye Dick."

Richard picks up a rock, catches up to Preston and whacks him over the head. Preston falls to the ground.

Fast as lightening, Shelly and Mina react. Mina crouches by Preston, keeping sand from obstructing his breathing. Shelly stabs Richard's eye with a stiff hand. She inflicts enough pain causing him to haunch, holding his right eye. He opens himself up to Shelly's next move, which ensues by picking up the same rock that struck Preston to bat that ass. Before she can do so, Tim and Jim wrestle Shelly to the ground. They keep Shelly at bay without being overly violent.

While Tim and Jim implore Shelly to calm down, Preston lies motionless, smited unconcious. He has a flashback. His dream envisions arms driving iron stakes into the ground around a pond. Each stake has a chain attached to it. The other ends are thrown in the water. Preston's father instructs the crew with the assemblage. Preston's father has a red flag in his left hand. His other hand holds a line, he begins backing up. The line tugs the chains and his crew squats once Preston's father waves the red flag. When he drops the flag, both hands hold the main line. He runs ten steps to the right and ten steps to his left. Simultaneously, all chains in the water tighten. Stakes bend and flex. One stake snaps and hits a worker on his side temple, instant fatality. Preston's father reinforces remaining stakes using a sledge hammer which he then tangles to the main line. This enables the hammer to become a useful handle.

No longer moving left to right, Preston's father refuses to loosen his grip. He continues the tug of war. The assistants yell, "Stop, let go!" The leader of the pack does no such thing. His intrepid grip on life drags him completely submerged in dark water. The lackeys on shore loiter stunned. Moments pass. A few start gathering equipment. All that's left of their leader are bubbles and swirls in the pond's murky water. The workers leave but one stays behind hollering at the group, "Where ya' goin'?" Five workers left the scene. A single friend of Preston's father remains circling the pond. This person has short auburn hair attributing forearms resembling Popeye. An onlooking stranger could surmise this loyal follower exhibiting a compassionate voice has soulful sentiment. So she stays. Soon after a minute, thrashing appears in the water. Everyone else long gone, she stands excitedly.

Preston's father catapults out of water. Resembling a heavy rag doll, he hits the ground with much force. The lone woman sprints to her leader's aid. He's beat up. His throat was slashed and face now unrecognizable. Grabbing his hand, she tears cloth from her waist to wipe his bloody forehead. He points upwards at the moon. She tearfully says, "Yes, that's where ya' goin'." The choking, dying man expresses, "No, make no use of the full moon." She pleads, telling him to hold on responding, "Never again. Boss, we don't even know if this damn thing is mortal." He brings the left arm he used to point at the dark sky over his body and opens up the palm…showing thick fur with sanguinary roots.

Mina runs to Shelly's boat nearby. She quickly fetches a small bucket, scoops up some sea water and throws the fill on Preston's face. He sits up, coolly gazing at Mina. Mina shrugs off his stare down. She returns the bucket. Richard and his cronies left the scene awhile ago. The entire time, Richard held his eye tight while shaking his fist and hitting his own thigh. Shelly (only one standing) questions Preston,

"Why turn your back on what you do not trust?"

Preston replies getting up,

"How bout' we go see Soundtrack?"

Mina joyfully claps her hands, stands on her tip toes and kicks the dirt. Dirt and sand go flying. Mina gets the party going. She sprints to their boat on shore. Made of wood, about ten to twelve feet long three feet wide enough. She always tries to nudge the boat off shore but never succeeds. After a few pushes she gives up, hops on board to speedily reel in the line connected to the anchor. Mina can do that laboriously. The anchor weighs twice as much as the child so that task keeps her busy until Preston and Shelly join in. Preston climbs on just in time. He helps Mina finish bringing anchor over the rail, possibly avoiding a catastrophic injury to the foot or toe. Shelly puts the bow of the ship at her right shoulder. She digs both feet into sand and shoves her ship into the water, smiling and waves goodbye. Preston and Mina laugh. Shelly does this joke often, acting as if she will not be leaving. She plunges into the water, swims as a fish, easily making her way on deck.

Roughly twenty yards out, the ship and noble crew of three linger for adjustments. Each has their own routine. Preston does nothing. He stands center peering at the sky, birds or whatever. Mina writes on scrap paper using charcoal. She takes this task seriously. She writes down one thing then gazes upward, intensely pondering and snapping her finger at every good thought to jot. Shelly takes out a cone. Yes...a cone. A wooden tool she puts in the water. Imagine a cheerleader's megaphone made of wood but Shelly Jibson's no cheerleader. She uses this device by having the small side up to her ear. The other circular wide end goes in the water. This commences the beginning of her routine which consists of listening intently. The second Shelly starts harkening, Preston stares waiting for a sign of direction. She puts a front side finger up to express wait one second. Everyone on deck knows the moment Shelly's face changes from serious to a simper, the day will be fruitful. If the wooden megaphone comes out of the water, without a smile from Shelly... well the day will be waisted. The hand holding a single finger up changes to a jubilant fist. The megaphone quickly exits the water. Shelly stands while carelessly dropping the tool. She points west with her hips and finger. Mina and Preston mimic Shelly's spontaneous gesture. Each adding their own shimmy. Oars raised by all three, now they have their heading.

Shelly stands shoulder to shoulder with Preston at center. Mina gives Shelly the scrap of paper. Shelly reads aloud Mina's notes: "Cinnamon, chocolate, nutmeg, mint and paprika. I'm not sure Soundtrack will have paprika, but I'll ask." The three paddle for an hour targeting a small landmass out of sight. Near the landmass, a wooden rickety boat floats. Music becomes louder as they advance toward the vessel. In the middle of the deep blue sea, an unusual rock formation sticks out of the water. This harbors a solitary person known to the group as Soundtrack. They found Soundtrack then and now by loud music and/or aquatic clicks.

Closing in on the raft, a large spray from a whale spews their starboard side. Then another at port-side. Whales breach and circle Shelly's ship. The spray from all the whales begin to take its toll on the crew. Mina loves it! She plays in the downpour everytime although nearly drowning the crew and sinking the canoe. A vociferous bang emits from Soundtrack's raft. Following a few more chest pounding thuds, the spray stops and always does cease on Soundtrack's cue. The boats now side by side, Mina ties a line connecting Shelly's boat to Soundtrack's. Prior to jumping on board other boat, Shelly addresses Preston asking, "Same as usual?" Preston replies, "I hope so."

Shelly leaps onto Soundtrack's big wobbly deck. Preston and Mina stay behind and wait. Shelly knocks on the door in a rhythmic beat. The door opens. A cloud of smoke pours out. Shelly enters (Song "Drift Away" by Dobie Gray plays loudly). A plank for a door closes. Preston and Mina hear Shelly's boisterous laughter. After an hour passes the door swings open. Shelly's coughing and carrying a sack on her back like Santa. She skips off Soundtrack's boat and joins Preston and Mina. Shelly hands Mina fabric, "Good news, good news, Mina." Shelly looks at Preston in a serious manner. She gives Preston a folded note and says, "Tidings from Kingmon." Preston reading the note, "This isn't good, this is not good." Shelly tosses a smaller sack similar to a coin pouch which lands in his lap. He grabs the pouch and sniffs the contents.

He smiles and puts the pouch in his pocket. Shelly tells Preston,

"I think that will lift your spirits" and Preston conveys, "Okay…so not a horrible day."

Preston glimpses over to Mina and Shelly,

"We sure do love Soundtrack, don't we?"

Mina quickly responds,

"Yeah!"

Preston was given word he must confer with Kingmon today. Hence Shelly, Mina and Preston make their way to eerie Bantam Island. Approximately three leagues east by sundown they should arrive. In the meantime Mina happily sifts and sorts through her cherishable goody bag. Shelly seems worrisome. Preston keeps his eyes fixed on due course praying silently to arrive before sundown… and so they do. Preston gets hasty. He desires not to have this obligatory conference among the dark.

Mina tosses the anchor over with assistance from Shelly. They are about twenty yards off the coast of Bantam Island - a dwelling for a king and his carnivorous bantams. A gentle current along with a sandy beach makes an easy swim for Preston. He walks slowly on shore, his haste decreases. He studies the trees, repeatedly glancing over his shoulder. He begins sweating as he comes upon a giant iron door. Preston takes a deep breath, knocks three times on a haven's door with his fist. He backs up as the large door opens wide moving dirt, rock and sand. The door dwarfs Preston when he moves forward the door closes. The trees are plentiful, unlike any seen these days. Variable types of fruit and nut trees but that's not all; no woman or man goes out on a limb in these trees. Preston continues down the path. The branches shake violently. He immediately stops gazing up in awe at the fruit. He dare not touch. Then screeching and yowling pervades. Preston's scared. He feels this could be his last visit. A shadow ahead freezes him. Preston squints and puts a hand over his brow to block the setting sun. In a karate stance, Preston braces himself for what's approaching him quickly down the path. He is relieved. The four legged figure presents itself as a gray canine wearing a playful smile. The dog shakes off its coat, sending water on Preston and he smiles too; happy to see Dank the dog. Preston reaches in his pouch for one of Soundtrack's treats.

Preston tosses one in Dank's mouth. He continues down the path with Dank. The trail gradually becomes more narrow, then rocks on both sides make up a natural barrier.

A cedar door protrudes from the encased surrounding stone. Dank pouts, then a little cry as the dog backs up. Preston fluffs out vines next to the door. He grabs hold of the clapper. Dank bolts. Another deep breath, Preston rings a bell covered by foliage. Every limb shakes from the trees above. A long drawn out howl creates a dreadful cacophony of primate sounds. Not shameful to disclose, Preston's legs shake in terror. This physically fit, properly proportioned individual can barely stand, let alone endure the scary dark venue. The door opens vertically, he hesitates. Almost as if someone put a heavy weight on Preston's sandal. He manages to muster his first step forward. The rocky path comes to an end. A dead-end.

Steps stop Preston's route. Big stone steps, something the Mayans and Aztecs would approve of.

The trees cease turbulence. Preston wipes his forehead with the back of his hand and then again with the other hand. He clears his throat in preparation to greet verbally but a descending chink interrupts. A coin falls hitting each step on the way down. The bronze coin halts at Preston's feet. Using a dexterous foot, he flicks it up to his hands. He catches the coin and tosses it to catch again in his other hand. Preston announces,

"A fine day to see such a king! What do you make of this?"

A heavy walking stick helps a life-force move from its spot up top. Two bare feet adorned with hula skirts stand up, booming a voice down the steps. Walking while talking, Kingmon descends from his floral throne responding,

"Man, man and his lavish waste."

Preston nods,

"Agreed."

Kingmon acknowledges,

"Agreed, I like that."

The king appears to be in good spirits as he nears Preston. Lording over on the final step, Kingmon places a hand on Preston's shoulder questioning,

"How are you, nephew?" Kingmon and Preston trot along a game trail. Preston speaks, "What brings me here today?"

Kingmon treads heavily. He covers himself using palm leaves - also shields his forearms and shins with arboreal bark. Kingmon sports a makeshift cap as well, palm leaves decorated by adding fresh flowers every day. The brown vegetation atop blocks kingmon's face entirely. The two come to an opening on this island's forest. Kingmon and Preston loiter in the middle of this clearing. The sun has set. Darkness prevails. Dreadful silence looms as Kingmon stares at Preston. Light from a torch held by Kingmon shines a giant shadow on the tall trees.

Back on the boat, Shelly does her best to sleep off an empty stomach. Mina has a desire to see these legendary bantams for herself.

Testing the sleepy mate, Mina gently nudges Shelly. No smack-back, Mina jumps off the ship and runs. She sprints down the shore to be stunned by that giant iron door. She goggles up in awe of its size and impenetrable appearance. Instead of flipping out and hitting the door, Mina props herself up, leaning on a tree nearby. She witnesses a sweet sight. Fruit dangles from most limbs. A rarity, the last piece of fruit she savored was months ago…a birthday gift from Soundtrack. Thus she climbs high up, snags a delectable mango steep in the trees. She enjoys. Noticing her advantageous height now, Mina bravely goes out on a limb and crosses over to the tree's tall neighbor. She grooves her way down safely, going over the seemingly impervious entrance.

All the while Kingmon still stares at Preston. Preston, throwing his arms, blurts with deliberate request,

"Well get on with it!"

Kingmon responds quietly and moves closer to Preston muttering,

"We need one."

Preston, looking at Kingmon,

"Can't do it."

Kingmon puts his stick in the ground and shakes his head. Preston continues,

"Can't do it. I trade spices, crops and goods. Not humans."

Kingmon retorts,

"Then why are you here? Why are you the exception? You can easily become the one."

Preston expresses,

"I am the exception because my father taught you that beast can die."

Kingmon sharply replies,

"You have been given dispensation because of your mother, not your father. Your father was one of the prodigal ones." Preston, holding back his frustration,

"You don't have news for me…do you Kingmon?"

Again Kingmon places a hand on Preston's shoulder. The grasp becomes a tighter grip causing Preston to wince. Kingmon, being stronger, brings Preston to his knees by squeezing his neck and collar. Preston grabs hold of Kingmon's forearms, fighting for some slack. A drum beat from the surrounding woods begins. Boom… boom, the constant drumbeat sounds while Preston wiggles for Kingmon to relent. The ominous beat changes its rhythm. Shadows show themselves in the trees. Dark forms holler, encompassing the forest clearance. Those shadows climb down. Not a couple but hundreds perceivable. The numerous others on the outer perimeter are made larger and more frightening in Preston's mind. Drums hit their highest level. Preston does what he can to fight free but Kingmon's grip has turned into a grapple.

Mina picks up the sound of drums. She sprints to the music close by finding the source at the opening where Kingmon detains Mina's father figure. Mina can't detect the sight of a struggle, she listens to the euphonious drumbeat. She begins jiving with the rhythm. Kingmon's torch staked into the sandy surface illuminates a young girl dancing as if there is no tomorrow. Stunned by this groovy surprise, Kingmon loosens his grip on Preston. Preston catches his breath on the ground. When the beat adds notes, Kingmon stands watching Mina dance her heart out.

Kingmon takes notice of his spooky bantams getting closer without attacking. All have climbed down making it clear the sound of drums emanates from each bantam. For every bantam holding a sharp stone there be a bantam drumming the hell out of a banjo. They are furry, short and muscular. For the first time their caretaker (Kingmon) witnesses his creatures smile by watching exuberant Mina busting moves to the sound that makes everybody else quiver.

Culminating to a climatic end, Mina finishes her last move on the final beat. She falls on the sand exhausted, not even curious of its source or reason. The shadows fade away howling contently. Preston hears Mina's sound of exhaustion and relief, inquiring in the dark, "Mina, that you?"

Kingmon approaches Mina with torch in hand. Preston stands and moves along side Kingmon's light. Preston feels no need to worry. The way Kingmon peers at Mina, its obvious his attitude has changed. Kingmon gives Preston the torch as Kingmon helps Mina up. On his knees, Kingmon questions Mina as would a gentle grandpa,

"Small one, where did you learn to dance like that?"
Mina gasping for air places a finger in kingmon's face gesticulating to hold a moment. Mina answers,

"My friend, Shelly."
Kingmon pries,
"You know Shelly Jibson?"
Mina nods her head twenty times as she bites her bottom lip. Kingmon erect, turns himself 180 degrees searching for his walking stick. Mina sweetly pokes Kingmon in the butt with what he searches for.

Kingmon snags his stick from Mina, flicks the coin at Preston and states,

"Well, seems you have a new commodity but this one isn't for consumption…my regards to Shelly Jibson." Kingmon leaves the area. Preston murmurs to Mina,

"Thanks for saving my behind." Mina giggles. Preston holds up the coin to the full moon's luminance, puts it in his sleeve suggesting to Mina,

"Let's get out of here."
Preston and Mina safely return to Shelly and the boat. On the way back, Shelly doesn't speak a word. Neither does Mina or Preston but anchoring ashore, post an hour trip to ulterior islands, Mina pulls Shelly by the waistband asking,

"Why aren't you curious?
Kingmon says, hey!"
Shelly recommends Mina not to be excited, leaning in to whisper,
"Want to know a secret?"
Mina hangs on Shelly's next words,
"Kingmon's a snake."
Mina stays on boat. Shelly along with Preston alights. After a short moment mulling over Shelly's statement, Mina jumps off too following the group.

The trio walking off beach, onto dirt and around some rocks surrounded by thorn bushes freeze the population of fifty or so. Make shift tents (made by trees which once dominated the island) shelter these invasive inhabitants. Not one tree left standing, swaying nor fruiting. All family trees were chopped down to be burnt, giving birth to an innate problem inflicted on this marooned town. All crops consumed, none managed to cultivate in order to reap. They are always hungry and thirsty. So that's why all eyes are on Shelly and Preston.

Mina mingles with several children. Everyone encroaches Shelly and Preston on their way into their hut. They ask,

"What you got for us? See anything out there?"

The grilling never lets up. Anytime the three leave to explore or gather, harassment ensues when they return. Shelly was the only one of the colonials to have the sense to fabricate a raft from the wood. Years went by, and so did Preston, backing up her idea. Bearing numerous cold nights building a floating vessel. Now that the villagers depleted all resources; Shelly's ridiculed idea has substance. Weeks went by watching from shore as Preston, Mina and Shelly made lumber ship shape and sea worthy by hollowing out a large tree trunk.

Since they always paddle out of sight, the people desire to know what's out there as much as they crave food. Shelly has a special way of fending off the human scavengers. She's cool for fifty yards out. Once she closes in on ten feet, Shelly must be aggressive upon entering her area. They tug and poke thus Shelly stokes thrashing the encircling pack with the most formidable weapon around - a sword. Throwing their arms up conceding, the gaggle backs up and simmers down. Shelly stands firmly showcasing her blade's every angle. This clears the path for Preston to enter. The last person that shoved Preston while entering the tent was slashed on the wrist by the one and only Shelly.

Without hesitation Shelly follows Preston. They sit and wait for the crowd outside their hut to scatter. When the coast is clear, they hydrate themselves from stashing fresh water in a covered hole into the earth. On a previous venture, Mina spotted copper jugs on white

caps one windy day. They possess a secret luxury. A luxury material-
ized by generations before; however, eradicated by mother nature's
rising sea levels.

Silence among the people has Shelly and Preston wonder. The
two sip on water while contemplating the unusual absence of chatter.
Ten minutes pass when Mina's voice breaks the silence. Preston and
Shelly hear Mina scream,

"Stop! You goof! Get off!"

The two fire out of their spot. They see Richard has Mina by
the arm. Tugging the hell out of her, Richard shakes Mina violently.
He stops when Shelly and Preston show true intentions of physical
malice. Shelly angrily enunciates, "What's the problem Dick?" Mina
stands behind her two pals with a broken spirit. Richard points at
Mina declaring,

"This tyke here knows more than the two of you!"

Shelly and Preston speaking simultaneously,

"Yep. That's right."

Preston adds,

"Dick, why does this anger you?" Richard took a posy from Mina's
pocket. He grips the bloom with his fist crumpling blossoms. Richard
leers at Preston,

"Show me where these flowers grow."

Preston says firmly,

"I can't do that Dick."

Richard rushes at Preston. They fall to the ground rustling. They
thrusts sloppy throws as the two roll around in the dirt. Tim and Jim
break up the fight.

Shelly's more disgusted by the expression of satisfaction on everyone's face than the childish behavior conducted. Preston stands up
fast insisting,

"It is crucial no one step on that island. We must follow this rule
to survive."

Richard eases up deceitfully, glides over to Mina,

"I am sorry I hurt your arm little girl."

Richard collars Mina close to him at the waist,

"Show me the island or I will wring her neck."

Mina begins to wiggle vigorously for extrication. Shelly breaks out yelling at the top of her lungs,

"Okay Dick, we will go right now! Okay. Okay, we will go now. Release Mina."

Richard releases Mina. Mina runs to Shelly and Preston. Richard grins as would a serpent, happily stating,

"That's it! Wasn't so bad."

The villagers instantly become excited with thoughts of resources to come soon. Preston speaks to Richard, "Get your boat and men ready."

Richard waves over Tim and Jim. They head to their makeshift vessel. Years ago Shelly carried out her plan of constructing a small ship using a tree on the island. While doing so, Richard paid attention but by no means would take part or help - instead he copied her. Stealing wood from others to put together what's barely able to keep afloat, let alone accommodate three numbskulls who covet the ship always safely guarded by Shelly Jibson and her trustworthy entourage. Gathering on shore the entire village anxiously spectates. They have been told for years about what lives on the out of sight islands that folklore calls...Monster Island also known as Devil's Garden. A place laden with vegetation and fruits. Shelly has the raft to venture that far. Generations before villagers, including Preston's father and Shelly's mother had a ship capable of accomplishing the trek but an uncivil war broke out destroying the only boat around.

Richard has his raft far away from Shelly's. He knows his boat will seem silly next to Shelly's. Richard and his posey push off using a large stick. The colony waves goodbye to the three a few yards away from shore. They begin raising the only sail on their flotation device. The task of hoisting creates friction among those obtuse gangsters. Richard slaps Jim's wrist. Richard smacks Tim over the head causing Tim to drop a map. Then Richard furiously pulls the main line finally completing the simple goal of raising one sail five feet. From contentment, Richard stomps his foot while taking control of the vessel's rudder. Tim rubs the top of his head and glares at Richard gloating. Tim jumps off board to fetch his importantly handed down map in the water. He's close enough and swims back to shore. He blends with the colony and immediately lifts the map high up above his head, shaking it similar to a polaroid picture.

Beside Preston Mina laughs. Preston stops Mina,

"Now, that's it! What are you laughing at?"

Shelly eyes a mesquito on her shoulder, she slays then flicks her shoulder wondering too,

"Yeah, what is it?"

Mina cops a serious attitude. She has their attention and scans around to be certain no villager can hear. Mina opens up,

"No one said anything about the flowers I brought. Got us into trouble but no one mentioned the beauty of the blue!" Preston jibes,

"Okay you are right. I saw them in the corner of my eye and I failed to tell you how pretty they were."

Mina smiles waggling her eyebrows disclosing,

"That's more like it! Now I can tell you...they are posionous."

Mina chortles again. From there the three blend with congregating crowd on shore. Mina gets tagged by a youthful peer sending her running away. Preston and Shelly stare at Richard a few yards out with Jim. Shelly whispers to Preston,

"There's no wind."

Preston titters covering his mouth.

On board Richard's vessel, Jim points decisively in the westward direction. Richard still circles going nowhere making the hulk in the water a joke.

The colony's laughter hits Richard like a punch in the face. He stands leering at everybody laughing at him. Richard jumps off his poor excuse for a boat, drags it by the bow to shore. He tramps his way to Preston and Shelly...face to face, Richard orders Preston,

"Tomorrow! You and I go first thing tomorrow!"

Richard scratches vehemently, he had more to scream about but his hand and foreaem drive him crazy. He rolls up his right sleeve to scratch then starts tugging at his trousers. Shelly horns in,

"Something wrong Dick? Got ants in your pants?"

Going back to campsite Richard states firmly again,

"Tomorrow!"

The day coming to a close, so does the energy. The villagers heading for the bedding,

Shelly with Preston stretch and yawn pretending to be sleepy. They dally behind the crowd.

The crafty pair gain enough ground to separate themselves from the people. Preston's first to the canoe, Mina darts out of the woods right behind him. Ready to paddle and go; Mina and Preston desire Shelly to hurry up. Shelly lagged further behind sneaking inside her hut and careful to not make any noise. She slowly removes a piece of wood in the dirt, unearthing a small wooden barrel. Shelly replaces the wood, throws dirt back over, composes herself and nonchalantly exits. Moving at a fast rate but not too rapid, Shelly doesn't want to cause a stir. Luckily not harassed, she gets on board.

Preston rows as if his life depends on paddling. Mina ogles at the unfamiliar barrel Shelly has by her feet, while Shelly also paddles vigorously. Arriving within hours, Shelly and Preston guide their swift canoe onto the sandy shore of Devil's Garden. This legendary place has been stepped on by humans only several times. They are miles away from commoners on the desolate, stripped island. Palm trees everywhere. Ducks and geese play on a huge pond. The mythical pond of Rosa. Legend has a demonic beast lives underneath the pacific surface. Preston dreads entering the vast area laden with: grass, flowers, insects, rabbits, squirrels, deer roaming wildly and growing freely. Preston's father died somewhere along the fresh water's edge. Shelly fears not. Already on sand she encourages Mina (standing on canoe) by slapping the side of her thigh. Mina takes a deep breath. She locks eyes with Shelly which gives her the courage to keep up.

Shelly adjusting the barrel in her arms quirks her head at Preston, non verbally instructing the way. Preston reluctantly follows. The second he catches up, Shelly stabs the barrel with her bronze sword. Purple juice squirts out. Shelly lifts the container above her head swilling wine. She turns barrel over stopping the flow and puts her mouth over the made opening, repeating the process again more conservatively. After a couple of burps, Shelly saunters toward the pond's edge of pebbles and hurls the barrel into body of water. Mina and Preston are behind a boulder watching as Shelly comes back to sit beside them.

Shelly sets the mood, hands Mina and Preston a piece of jerky. Shelly sits on the ground and masticates. Preston chews wondering as he swallows and smacks his satisfied tongue asking, "Okay, so what now?" Shelly stands dusting off her hands. She takes Preston easily by the shoulder swallowing heavily before responding,

"Watch…wait for it."

At that very moment, the floating barrel jerks left then right. A spiraling eddy churns in the water, emerging a monster. A creature with hairy forearms, lifts the barrel above the water's surface. The hands dwarf the barrel as the beast grips the container how humans do a drinking can and wades out. Shaking off the water similar to a dog, the giant ape guzzles down the strong wine. The hairy primate snuffles the air, turning its head sharply at the group. They tuck behind the boulder before being spotted.

After a minute Preston furtively sneaks another peek. The beast lies comfortably on the dirt scratching. Mina can't move. Shelly sitting astride seriously tends to Mina's matted hair, she glances at Preston - then smiles. She has never seen that look on his face. Mina reaches her arms out for Preston to come and sit down. He does so, thinking aloud, "So what now?" Shelly grooming Mina's head retorts, "Wait."

Preston bobs his head as would a chicken, views around before rashly speaking,

"Wait for what?"

No response from Shelly drags out another line of questioning,

"What are we gonna' do about Richard? And, what do we do when this thing wakes up?"

Mina helps ease the tension by handing the fretting male a root to suck on,

"Here its ginger, it'll calm you down."

Preston accepts but doesn't let go of not being in the know,

"So what's up Shelly?"

Shelly consummates her duty as hairdresser, she stands up to address Preston,

"Go get the fishing net."

Preston confused, knowing the fishing net trolls on sea water,

"Now's not the time for fishing, sharks are out."

Shelly explains,

"We're fishin' here tonight."

Preston's face goes from perplexed to tortured. No blame on Preston. His father died here. For a lifetime villagers passed down horrific stories of how grisly the death was. Mina on the other hand bounces, kicking each leg outwards. A common dance routine when Mina gets excited...she's excellent at fishing.

Preston obliges walking away from pond area, back to the boat. He takes his time because Preston really hates that place. Although beautiful, this Island of the beast gives Preston the creeps. Shelly startles Preston retrieving net from the canoe. She runs up behind him suddenly with a poke on the back,

"Hey."

Preston jumps a little naturally but relief kicks in seeing Shelly. Shelly takes net in order to sincerely express,

"I know this place. My mother taught me some things before she died and she wanted your father's men to carry out our plan but they brushed her aside. Preston take my word, listen to me and this eden will be yours to reside."

Preston nods agreeably. The two go back to where they were with Mina.

Mina's gone. Both worried to death at her absence, they call out quietly,

"Mina, Mina, Mina."

Nowhere to be found. Nervousness sets in but they don't panic. Shelly freezes instantly.

She has become sick to her stomach. Oh my! She thinks, what happened? Preston slowly takes a gander around boulder barrier, spots Mina skipping pebbles in the water. Preston tells Shelly a few yards away,

"I see her, she's by the pond." A sight that would usually madden the couple if not for their newly grown sentiment. Asking while advancing timidly,

"Where is it?"

Without a care in the world Mina points,

"It went that way, yawning."

Shelly declares,

"Alright we can begin."

Preston leans toward Shelly,

"What about Richard?"

Shelly kind of frustrated quips back,

"Really? Just drag the line in. Forget about him. Let's take care of our hunger."

Mina knows the drill. They've been fishing here before. Preston would always forage on the west end of this rich island. Tonight he feels different. Preston stands firmly by the pond's shore. Mina reaches out for the net. At this time he usually hands over the net and retreats to gather fruits and nuts. Shelly and Mina do the fishing. Nevertheless, Preston stared a long time spying on that creature. Before he tucked away against the boulder, he locked eyes with it. The animal didn't come charging around the corner to kill them all. In fact, Preston can't help knowing deep down that so called "beast" has goodness within.

Mina encroaches Preston standing. She tugs net. He doesn't let go. The full moon shines brightly above the pond. Somehow he sees more clearly, feels more serene but the greatest newfound impulse here...Preston wants to get in the water. Mina stops tugging. She furrows her eyebrows dubiously at Shelly. Shelly's expression tells another story, she loves Preston's hungry eyes so she suggests,

"Go ahead, cool off, take the main line wit' you."

Mina places clinched fists on each hip declaring sarcastically,

"Fine, that's fine." Mina goes skipping along to explore. Shelly holds rope on shore connected to the net which Preston has entering the water. The Pond of Rosa stretches one hundred yards each way. Fish colonize the pond. Plants underwater and littoral flourish. Shelly sits down holding the rope tightly. Preston swims to middle of the pond. He sinks the net using rocks.

Richard wakes up early morning. He immediately storms out of his tent scanning for Tim and Jim. Jim sleeps right outside just how a loyal canine would. Richard rhetorically gibes, "Wanna go for a ride?"

Jim erects himself rubbing his eyes as he recommends subtly,

"We should eat."

Richard treading briskly away shouts,

"Come on, we'll eat in The Devil's Garden!"

Richard notices Shelly's tent isn't covered by drapes on the entry door. He runs over to poke his nose inside, finds out she's gone and darts from campsite. Jim follows lazily. Richard steps on the sandy shore of the commoner's barren island. Preston doesn't have his clothes hanging on the canoe. The canoe and crew seem to have awaken earlier. Jim comes up beside Richard glaring angrily in the direction of where Shelly, Preston and Mina moor their vessel. Richard flushes beet red, even shaking from bubbling wrath. Unlike any tone used, Richard curls his lips showing teeth,

"Let's get those damn dastards!"

Richard tramps to his boat with Jim dragging behind. Richard has both arms out moving towards what appears to be his boat,

"Where is the sail dummy?"

Tim stands on modified raft,

"We don't need them, genius! Here, take a paddle. I broke the boom for three. We gonna do it how they do it. I spied on dem' traitorous traders last night. They do what they do by all three of dem' rowing like bats out of some kinda' hell hole... understand?"

Richard and Jim climb on board curbing laughter.

A productive night of fishing has Preston digesting while lying beside Shelly sharpening her blade with help from a stone. Mina returns from her venture across the island. Folding both arms inwards, Mina brings back with her: almonds, cashews, peanuts, papaya and figs. Taking papaya Preston asserts,

"Huh...the figs are early this year."

The past year these three have come to this island every other week to gather just enough of what's richly abundant here: fruits, nuts, grass and occasional animal. Preston, Shelly and Mina have a heart and history with those who inhabit Commoner's Island. Therefore they sacrifice cloying themselves; giving out bits to anyone and everyone. Lately the people have grown desperate. They besiege and nag about always wanting more. Shelly knew this day would dawn when nothing remains on the once lush landscape of Commoner's Island.

Thirty or so made it out alive when the deluge came some centuries ago. Only a few peaks of landmass reach above the high surface of the Earth's ocean. The ones with knowledge of the sea (controlling a boat) rode out the flood. The popular island has been decimated after two hundred years by majority of survivors. Shelly spoke of this day. She told everyone years ago to chop down only one tree.. those that don't fruit nor harbor life. Shelly said tactfully,

"Leave the rest alone, live off the sea."

No one listened to her words of wisdom.

Mina drops her load. She exclaims before sprinting away,

"I saw grain!"

Shelly's mouth starts salivating. Preston sleeps next to the fire belting out sounds of satisfaction. Shelly for the first time in her arduous existence - feels great happiness. Her eyes water. She smiles from ear to ear and releases the sword she has gripped tightly for too long.

Richard's fervent group, sculling in the same direction, lose their target. They stop rowing. Their momentum escapes. Richard stands and throws down his paddle irately,

"Where they at? I can't push all day!"

Tim puts map in the air. He tilts his head while touching his chin emitting the classic,

"Hmmm?"

Jim spots smoke on the near horizon. He blurts,

"There!"

All three snap back to paddling, anon they gaze at the mythical Monster Island. An island said to behold Earth's greatest spoils; most importantly a body of fresh water. Rainwater slakes the throat, sluices the skin; but man oh man what yearning we have for our own eden. They gain steam by imagination and greed.

Richard's canoe slams on shore, killing a crab. All three jump ship. Richard saved his last bit of snuff for this moment. He reaches for the back pocket in his favorite coat. Already craving intensely, Richard starts spitting. He fidgets and changes attention to another pocket. He notices the pocket holding his tobacco has a missing button. He reaches in, feels nothing, pulls the pocket inside out. There are no contents because no button secures his pacifier. Anger sets in again. Instead of tobacco, Richard ejects a thick ball of phlegm onto the pristine shore. Jim alleviates himself on a floral bush, flushing out pissed off butterflies. Tim and Jim target the smoke while Richard dawdles behind. Richard licks his lips scoping Mina picking grain.

A sleepy Preston has a dream about his mother. Must be this place or a sated stomach that gives Preston a vision of bathing. His mother pours water over his head. She towers the tub. Preston old enough to speculate,

"Where this from?"

One last spill over the head, rinsing Preston clean, his mother informs,

"Give thanks to God's creatures."

Shelly's moment of placidity stops. She hears footsteps. Her heart drops when she hears the sound of voices. Tim pops out of the woods. Shelly jumps up...zoning in on Tim. Jim comes up from behind Shelly and knocks her out with a rock. Sweet Shelly, she placed her sword next to Preston. He awakes from the commotion. His eyes immediately spot the bronze sword. As if spurred by divinity, he grabs the sword and spins around. Tim and Jim chuckle how hyenas do. Preston waves Shelly's sword from side to side goading,

"Get back, stay back!"

Unwholesome impulses urge Richard further through the field of grain. Undergoing a transformation, Richard's gait changes from curious to predatory. Mina hears something, her attention diverts from grain. She hears another groan. Mina tracks the sound of an animal. She stops to rest by a tree, in doing so she heeds a root system beneath her. She digs up a piece of root, cuts off her share with a stone, buries the rest. Richard didn't witness the act. He hasn't caught up to the scene but dogs twenty yards away.

The loudest yawn expelled close by has Mina spring up. She knows what she now searches for. The beast slumbers nearby. An amiss pile of sticks and brush compels Mina to creep slowly, minding each of her steps. Crawling on her hands and knees, Mina presently feels the breathing. A sleeping "monster" tucks away ten feet down a hole in the earth. Astonishment! Mina reaches for a fig to magnify the profound moment. The beast clears its throat causing Mina to tremble and drop the fig; the small fruit bops the creature on the head. The creature begins climbing up the side wall. Mina quakes all over except her left arm. She empties grain from a side pocket. She instinctively hopes to appease this beast crawling up the side of a hole. Mina's scared stiff. The beast opens its mouth, growling intensely vis-a-vis Mina.

Mina has sweetness stashed away for safe keeping. By the grace of God she's able to take out a treasured piece of chocolate. Instead of savoring the sweet morsel herself, Mina places the chunk of coca in the creature's slobbering mouth. Its shoulders relax. No more growling. The tension of Mina's stare down diminishes. The beast halts apparent aggression, swallows and licks its lips repeatedly. Mina smiles at this behavior. She talks,

"Chocolate."

The creature swallows followed by more licks by big lips, tough tongue and gruffly repeats, "Chocolate."

Mina rolls over in amazement.

Meanwhile Preston kept Jim and Tim away. They spot Richard and bring a burning log with them. Richard snatches the torch from Tim telling him,

"Get more."

The two hoodlums rifle through the fire pit. Preston ignores the human vultures and puts all effort into helping Shelly wake up.

Tim and Jim run back with flaming logs in each hand. Richard launches scorching wood directly on top of the beastly hole, nearly hurting Mina. She jumps back. More logs on place descend catching shrubs ablaze. Mina screams,

"No!"

The three men continue throwing hot rods. Mina runs for Preston and Shelly. She assists Preston on ground holding Shelly. Mina whips out the root she extracted, snaps it like a twig and places medicine up against Shelly's nostrils. Mina takes a whiff herself. Preston releases Shelly. He stands, picks up two rocks and marches his way to blaze. Without breaking stride, Preston approaches Tim. He bashes him over the head. Tim falls, he's knocked the fudge out. Jim picks up a rock too, demanding Preston to come at him,

"Come on you sack of..."

Preston throws a stone so quickly, Jim doesn't finish his foul sentence. Dazed and confused, Jim fumbles for another rock on ground. Preston advances swiping up log and clobbers Jim's big head.

Richard stays busy increasing the magnitude of fire, suffocating the beast. Richard calls out athwart rising flames to Preston,

"We got it! We got it now Preston!"

Preston, locked on Richard's eyeballs, circles raging fire. Richard keeps fueling fire, ripping shrubs from ground, tearing limbs and branches off trees. Preston goes around lunging viciously. Richard whips out a spear that's always strapped to his right leg; thrusting his sharp point he grazes Preston's face. Dodging Richard's first and possibly lethal jab, Preston recoils wisely. Preston inhales his deepest breath yet, widening his stance before attempting to strike again. Fiery earth erupts, sending embers everywhere.

A massive animal kindred to Bigfoot blasts out of its burning domicile. Rolling and screaming, the beast casts notes of anguish causing even Richard to grimace. One last stand, cooked flesh and hair fall from the longtime resident.

Wheezing for air, the stumbling creature points upwards when a damn spear pierces its juggler. The beast stares directly into Preston's eyes as it collapses backwards onto the Earth.

Richard saunters over and spits on the the corpse, "Filthy thing."

After nursing Shelly back to lucidity, Mina runs and slides on the ground coming to a stop next to the dead godsend. She weeps. Preston's heart breaks during Mina's show of sadness. Richard starts laughing. Mina spouts tearfully,

"You dick!"

Richard cold-heartedly retorts,

"Every village needs one."

Shelly's now on sight. She joins Preston's side sadly. Only Mina's crying can be heard while Tim and Jim come to. Both rubbing their craniums. No one speaks for a moment until Jim and Tim cheer. They pat Richard on the back.

Preston pauses no more. He questions Shelly beside him,

"Where's your sword?"

Shelly, kind of out of it drops her arms,

"Oh crap."

Preston claps softly,

"Well done head honcho. I believe a celebration's in order."

Mina heard what Preston unjustly said. She somberly lifts her head up clarifying,

"What?"

Preston firmly addresses Shelly,

"Shelly, do you perhaps have more wine to salute the Big Kahuna's crowning achievement?"

Richard perks his ears up at Preston's speech. He vainly relishes the sound of his new nicknames. Richard bites,

"Wine you say?"

Preston nods,

"Oh you bet bossman, come we will tell the others what you have done here."

Preston places his arm around Richard, escorting him to the vessel. Preston has Shelly come along. Tim with Jim stare at the smoky creature.

Mina's moved on from crying to sitting silently. She picks off embers and brushes the poor animal. Richard rips off some fruit, tucking nuts and a mango in his jacket.

The three make their way for Commoner's Island. Richard rows the fastest sitting abaft.

Shelly's at the bow of the canoe. She glances back at Preston, mouthing and gesticulating,

"What the hell we doin' here?"

Preston ignores, continues rowing.

A few hours later the three arrive with a populace awaiting. The villagers catch the bow as the canoe beaches. Everyone must know, Richard alights doling out mango and rains the crowd with an assortment of nuts. Preston and Shelly remain seated in canoe stalling, they peacefully migrate inland to camp area. Richard boasts as he divulges all swarming around. The villagers attention on Richard gives Preston and Shelly a spell to confer inside their hut. Shelly's first to converse,

"So…what you thinking?"

Preston's digging up soil,

"We're gonna' get em' drunk. Help me out with this hatch." Shelly beseeches,

"No…I'm saving this. Let's go back, find my sword and stab that Dick."

Preston implores, "We'll get more wine."

Shelly grumbles,

"Awe…okay, here move."

Shelly knocks the hinge. She lifts the small plank covering the hole. She excavates a thick glass bottle.

Richard tells everyone to rip their huts, disassemble structures on the island and fasten together rafts. A frenzy breaks out. Galvanized by Richard's speech, people gossip while tearing down tents. Shelly and Preston approach Richard busy flirting with two women at each side. Preston salutes,

"To our leader!"

Preston uncorks a buxom bottle of stout wine. Shelly holds her head down. She can't bear the sight of her prized libation being swigged by swine. Richard snatches the bottle, sending drops outwards going to waste. The murderous jerk turns the decanter upwards. He spills portions on his neck and chest. The guzzling makes Shelly break out,

"Okay! Let's go captain."

Richard stands on Shelly's boat announcing to the crowd,

"To Zion we go!"

Richard sips then belts out,

"Come, let's go!"

A few were able to construct a float beside Shelly' s vessel. Preston takes the middle seat, Richard sits at the bow and Shelly's at the stern on her canoe.

The boat made by a few villagers starts off floundering. They get the hang of rowing in sync mimicking the three ahead. Richard stops paddling. He desires to drink and salute the boat behind them catching up. As they glide by, Richard holds the bottle up high.

He points toward Monster Island shouting,

"Sally forth!"

Richard stumbles, rocking the canoe.

Shelly gazes behind her. Seeing nobody nigh, she drops her paddle. Preston stands and gestures for the bottle. Richard slaps Preston's hand away. Preston recommends,

"Allow me to serve you."

Richard laughs causing him to choke with a mouth full of wine. Richard leans over the bow vomiting. Shelly hurdles over middle seat using Preston's shoulder for support. She grabs the bottle from Richard's dangling hand and pummels his thick skull at the front tip of her boat...remaining wine pours over the bow. Shelly releases bottle to fall in the boat. She wipes her forehead with forearm,

"Have Kingmon finish this creep; he's been stuck in my crop long enough."

Another nimble group passes,

"Hey, what's wrong with Richard?"

Preston gets up. Possessing an empty bottle, he waves while slurring at rubberneckers. The group giggles. They think Richard became too intoxicated. The villagers continue on.

Shelly and Preston head for Bantam Island before anyone else comes along. After an hour of non-stop rowing, Shelly and Preston ease their canoe onto the shore of Bantam Island. The two lug Richard's lifeless body off the boat. Richard's schlepped in between Shelly and Preston. Both have an arm of Richard's around their neck as Richard's feet drag. His eyes open as Preston bangs on the iron door. The gigantic slab opens. They take a few steps in...trees shake from bouncing bantams. The duo toss Richard to the ground. Preston exclaims noisily,

"A gift to Kingmon and his bantams!"

Richard on ground cries out,

"A lifetime of friendship and this is how you repay me?"

Preston and Shelly departing, walk through the entrance. Before the door shuts, Preston flicks the coin at Richard. When the door closes, screams of Richard's agony mixes with the sounds of feeding bantams - causing Shelly and Preston to cringe going back to their boat. They return exhausted to Monster Island at sunset.

By now most of the population has arrived. Groups are tearing apart the landscape.

They pick anything and everything. A clique of villagers stand and watch Mina scatter flowers by the dead beast. One person kicks the bottom foot of the charred monster,

"That's it. Doesn't seem like much."

Mina hisses at such a remark. A woman standing over Mina has the nerve to comment furthermore,

"Oh Mina, don't be a wild child."

That's when the people see the pond of Rosa. Not one of them stop to appreciate.

They all rush for the water and splash in jubilation. Instantly villagers dip dirty clothes and rags into the water, uselessly rinsing what's practically garbage. Those not polluting the water, chop down trees and consume as much as possible similar to a plague of locusts.

Preston and Shelly go to Mina. They stand somberly, then respectfully place the beast on fabric, helping them to slide the body back to its hole. As carefully as they can, they put the creature to rest covering its hole with earth. Mina tops the layer with flowers she picked.

Preston and Shelly enter the water. Their demeanor different from others. The majority stop splashing and a few leave the pond. Tim urinates in the water. Jim joins him at the pond's outer-bank. A vortex swirls, ceasing the urinary streams. Tim and Jim step back. Preston and Shelly surface juxtaposed, simultaneously shake water off as animals do. Tim and Jim don't finish relieving themselves.

A little boy explores the woods of monster island. He runs and trips over a rock. Prostrated on ground this young lad lifts himself to his knees. He checks his waistband, its still there. He takes out an item, holding up a button to make certain. He smiles with a serpentine tongue getting up. His knee knocks a pommel. The boy sifts through dirt displaying Shelly's sword.

He drops the button and picks up the sword. He's sinisterly mesmerized by light reflecting off blade then stands creepily.

A couple of people gather belongings from floats on shore of Monster Island. The sun sets behind bantam island. A villager pokes an acquaintance, pointing at a landmass which has always been out of view - they gasp.

Back on Commoners Island, a fatigued sea turtle swims onto an empty shore...sets up shop in the sand to lay some eggs. A migrating flock of gannets descend from the sky. They immediately pick at left-over refuse. Later seeds of grass sprout and a new era begins.

www.ingramcontent.com/pod-product-compliance
Lightning Source LLC
Chambersburg PA
CBHW020610130626
46552CB00007B/3140